There was an old man named Joaquim who was the lighthouse keeper on the island of Santiago in Cape Verde off the West Coast of Africa. His friend, a young boy named Paulo, often stopped by the lighthouse on his way home from school. The lighthouse was a great place to visit: one could climb the tower and see the entire harbor with the beautiful boats at anchor; there were rocks at the point to dive from and the clear sea for swimming; sometimes Paulo just sat in the courtyard and Joaquim told stories.

But one afternoon the boy visited the lighthouse, slumped into a chair, and stared at his feet.

"Would you like to climb the tower?" the old man asked him.

"No," Paulo said morosely.

"How about a swim?" Joaquim offered, "It is a beautiful, clear day."

"I don't feel like swimming," Paulo replied.

"Then I can tell you the story of the time the light went out in the lighthouse," Joaquim said.

"I don't want to hear a story," Paulo told the old man.

"Well," the lighthouse keeper said, "we'll just sit then."

Paulo stared at his feet, his bottom lip trembled, and the boy began to cry.

"What is the matter, my friend?" the old man asked. Joaquim poured Paulo a glass of water.

The boy took a sip of the cool water and rubbed his eyes. "Something happened at school today," Paulo said.

The lighthouse keeper's face was dark brown and wrinkled from living so many years by the sea, but his eyes were lively and clear—a light, light-blue, almost silver in color. "What happened?" the old man asked.

Paulo chewed his bottom lip and rubbed his feet together. He took a deep breath and said, "Sara Mendez said that you were a silly old man and I pushed her down."

"Is she hurt?" Joaquim asked.

"She skinned her knee," Paulo said. "She was crying. I ran away."

Joaquim nodded his head and scratched the gray whiskers on his chin. He took a sip of water and poured another glass for Paulo. "What are you going to do?" the old man asked.

Paulo looked at the blue sea sparkling in the sun. "I want to hide," the boy said.

"What about talking to her?" Joaquim asked. "You could apologize."

"Apologize?" Paulo yelled. "She said you were silly!"

The old man chuckled and patted Paulo on the knee.

"Why are you laughing?" Paulo demanded.

"Because perhaps this girl, Sara Mendez, is right," Joaquim said. "Perhaps I am silly. I live all alone at the lighthouse and except for you, my friend, I only talk with the sea gulls."

"You are not silly!" Paulo shouted. "You make things and keep the ships safe in the storms!"

"Even so," the old man said in a serious tone, "you should not have pushed the girl." Joaquim leaned back in his chair, crossed his arms, and regarded the boy.

"I know," Paulo mumbled while looking down at his feet.

"Does she live in your village, Paulo?" the old man asked.

"Yes," Paulo replied, "just down the road."

"You cannot hide from her forever," Joaquim said. "Unless you become invisible," the old man added, "which seems unlikely." He chuckled slightly at this thought.

"But her older brother Miguel will kill me when he finds out!" Paulo said.

"Older brothers generally do not like it when people shove their sisters," Joaquim said, looking steadily at Paulo.

"What am I going to do, Joaquim?" Paulo asked desperately.

A slight breeze picked up off the ocean, ruffling the sleeves of the old man's shirt. "I think you should go to Sara Mendez's house and apologize to her."

"Will you go with me?" Paulo asked the old man.

Joaquim placed his hands on the table and leaned toward Paulo. "I will go with you as far as the girl's house," the old man said, "but you must knock on the door and talk with her by yourself."

The sun was beginning to set as Paulo and Joaquim walked out the front gate of the lighthouse. A warm breeze blew down from the highlands and swept a thin band of spray off the waves that broke along the shore. The old man rested his hand on the boy's shoulder as they walked.

When they reached the village, the first stars were twinkling in the blue-dark of the evening sky. Lights flickered on in the windows of the small houses. Some kids playing soccer by the light of a streetlamp stopped their game and watched Paulo and his old friend walk by.

"I will be right here," Joaquim said when they reached the front gate of Sara Mendez's house.

"O.K.," Paulo said.

The boy hesitated and then unlatched the gate. He smelled the family's dinner cooking and heard their voices inside the house as he walked up the path. Paulo glanced back at Joaquim. The old man was there, but he looked like nothing more than a shadow.

Paulo knocked on the door and Sara opened it.

She was wearing a pretty blue dress.

Paulo said, "I came to apologize for pushing you at school today, Sara." His voice was shaking.

Sara scratched her knee just above a large bandage with spots of blood on it. "Why did you get so mad about that silly old man?" she asked.

"He is not silly!" Paulo said angrily. He stopped himself. "I'm sorry," Paulo said. "The old man is my friend."

"I didn't know he was your friend," Sara said, "but you shouldn't have pushed me, Paulo."

"I know," Paulo said. "That was wrong."

"I'm sorry that I said your friend was silly, Paulo."

"It's O.K.," Paulo told her. "Maybe you will visit the lighthouse someday."

Sara laughed. "Maybe," she said, but it didn't seem like she wanted to.

"I hope your knee feels better," Paulo said.

"Thank you, Paulo."

"I'll see you tomorrow in school," Paulo said.

"O.K.," Sara told him. "I'll see you."

Paulo said goodnight and Sara closed the door. He walked back to the gate and met Joaquim.

"How do you feel?" the old man asked.

Paulo shut the gate to Sara's house and said, "I wish that I had not pushed her, but now that I have apologized I feel a little better."

The stars shone in the night sky as the old man and the boy walked down the street.

Vocabulary

P.13

chucklc [`tʃʌkl̩] v. 咯咯的笑

P.15

mumble [`mʌmbl̩] v. 咕噥著說

P.17

invisible [ɪn`vɪzəbl̩] adj. 看不見的

unlikely [ʌn`laɪklɪ] adj. 不太可能的

shove [ʃʌv] v. 推

P.19

ruffle [`rʌfl̩] v. 弄皺

P.20

highland [`haɪlənd] n. 高地 (常用複數)

P.23

flicker [`flɪkɚ] v. 閃爍；忽隱忽現

P.25

unlatch [ʌn`lætʃ] v. 拉開門閂

故事中譯

p.2

　　有個名叫喬昆的老人，在非洲西岸外海、維德角的聖地牙哥島當燈塔看守人。他的朋友——一個名叫保羅的小男孩——時常在放學回家的路上順道拜訪他。喬昆看守的燈塔是個值得參觀的好地方：你可以爬上塔頂，鳥瞰整座港口和停泊在那兒的美麗漁船；在海岬的尖端有幾處岩石可以跳水，還有清澈的海水可以游泳；有時，保羅就只是坐在庭院裡，聽喬昆說故事。

p.4

　　但是有天下午，男孩來到這座燈塔後，便一屁股坐在椅子上，低頭盯著他的雙腳看。

　　老人問：「你想要上去燈塔看看嗎？」

　　保羅悶悶不樂的說：「不想。」

　　喬昆提議：「那游泳好不好？今天天氣很晴朗呢！」

　　保羅回答：「我不想游泳。」

　　喬昆說：「那麼，我來說個有一次燈塔燈光熄滅的故事給你聽！」

　　保羅告訴他：「我不想聽故事。」

　　這位燈塔看守人說：「那好吧！我們也可以就這樣坐著。」

p.6

　　保羅盯著自己的雙腳，下唇顫抖著，接著就哭了起來。

老人問：「我的朋友，怎麼了？」他倒了一杯水給保羅。

男孩啜飲了一口清涼的水，揉揉他的雙眼，說：「今天在學校發生了一件事。」

ᵖ.8

這位燈塔看守人有著深棕色的臉龐，因為多年住在海邊而佈滿了皺紋，但是他的雙眼卻炯炯有神而且清澈──那是一種淺到近似銀色的灰藍。老人問：「發生了什麼事？」

保羅咬著下唇，兩腳不安的互相摩擦。他深呼吸了一口氣，然後說：「莎拉·曼德茲說你是一個笨老人！我很生氣，所以就把她推倒了。」

喬昆問：「她受傷了嗎？」

保羅說：「她的膝蓋擦傷了，哭了起來，然後我就跑走了。」

ᵖ.11

喬昆點點頭，搔了搔下巴上灰色的鬍鬚。他啜了一口水，然後又倒了一杯水給保羅，問他：「你打算怎麼辦？」

保羅凝視著在陽光下閃閃發光的藍色海洋。他說：「我想躲起來。」

喬昆問：「找她談談如何？你可以向她道歉啊。」

P.13

保羅大叫：「道歉？她說你是笨蛋耶！」

老人輕輕的笑了一笑，然後拍拍保羅的膝蓋。

保羅追問：「你為什麼還笑得出來？」

喬昆說：「因為，也許這位叫莎拉·曼德茲的女孩是對的。也許我的確是笨蛋。我獨自一個人住在燈塔裡，而且除了你之外，我的朋友，我只和海鷗交談。」

保羅大叫：「你才不笨！你會動手做東西，還讓漁船平安度過暴風雨！」

P.15

老人以嚴肅的口吻說：「即使如此，你也不應該推倒那個女孩啊。」他往後靠在椅背上，交叉雙臂，注視著男孩。

保羅低頭看著他的雙腳，喃喃的說：「我知道。」

老人問：「保羅，她住在你的村子裡嗎？」

保羅回答：「是的，就在路的另一頭。」

P.17

喬昆說：「你不可能永遠躲著她，除非你變成隱形人！」接著他又補上一句：「不過那似乎是不可能的。」他被自己的這個想法逗得咯咯笑。

保羅說：「但是她的哥哥邁高知道以後會殺了我的！」

喬昆沉著的注視著保羅，說：「做哥哥的通常都不喜歡別人推自己的妹妹。」

保羅絕望的問：「那我該怎麼辦呢，喬昆？」

p.19

一陣微風從海洋的遠方揚起，拂動老人的衣袖。「我認為你應該去沙拉・曼德茲的家向她道歉。」

保羅問老人：「你會陪我一起去嗎？」

喬昆將手靠在桌子上，傾身對保羅說：「我會陪你一起走到那女孩的家，但是你必須自己去敲門，然後和她談談。」

p.20

當保羅和喬昆從燈塔的前門走出來時，太陽正開始下山。一陣溫暖的微風從高地吹下來，掃過在岸邊散開的海浪，吹起細長的浪花。

一路上，老人一直將手搭在男孩的肩膀上。

p.23

他們到達村莊的時候，初現的星星已在傍晚暗藍的天空中閃閃發光。燈光在一間間小房子的窗內一一亮起。一群在街燈下踢足球的小孩子停下他們的遊戲，看著保羅和他年長的朋友經過。

當他們到達莎拉・曼德茲家的前門時，喬昆說：「我在這裡等你。」

保羅說：「好。」

p.25

男孩猶豫了一下，然後打開大門的門閂。當他走上小徑時，聞到了這家人煮晚餐的香味，並聽到屋子裡說話的聲音。保羅回頭看了看喬昆；他還是待在原地，不過看起來只是一團黑影。

保羅敲敲門，而開門的正是莎拉。

她穿著一件可愛的藍色洋裝。

p.26

保羅說：「莎拉，我來為今天在學校把妳推倒的事道歉。」他的聲音在顫抖。

莎拉抓了抓她裹著大繃帶的膝蓋上方，繃帶上還透出斑斑血跡。她問：「為什麼你會為了那個笨老人發這麼大的脾氣？」

保羅生氣的說：「他才不笨！」接著，他停了下來，說：「對不起。那個老人是我的朋友。」

莎拉說：「保羅，我不知道他是你的朋友。但你不該推我的。」

保羅說：「我知道。那樣做是不對的。」

p.28

「很抱歉我說你的朋友是笨蛋。」

保羅告訴她：「沒關係。也許妳可以找一天來參觀燈塔。」

莎拉笑了。她說：「也許吧！」但是她看起來似乎並不想去。

保羅說：「希望妳的膝蓋好一點了。」

「保羅，謝謝你。」

保羅說：「明天學校見。」

莎拉告訴他：「好，明天見。」

P.30

保羅向莎拉道過晚安後，莎拉關上了門。保羅走回前門和喬昆會合。

老人問：「你覺得怎麼樣？」

保羅關上莎拉家的前門，說：「我希望我沒有推過她，但是現在道過歉後，我覺得好一點了。」

老人和男孩一起走過街道，而星星正在夜空中閃爍著。

Exercises

Part One. Reading Comprehension

Answer the following questions about the story in short sentences.

1. What had happened to Paulo that day at school?
2. Why was Paulo so angry with Sara?
3. After hearing about what Paulo had done at school, what did Joaquim suggest to Paulo?
4. How did Paulo feel after apologizing to Sara?

Part Two. Topics for Discussion

Answer the following questions in your own words and try to support your answers with details in the story. There are no correct answers to the questions in this section.

1. Joaquim said in the story, "*Perhaps I am silly. I live all alone at the lighthouse and except for you, my friend, I only talk with the sea gulls.*" Judging from this statement, what kind of personality do you think Joaquim has?
2. Have you ever felt apologetic about offending someone? Did you make up for what you'd done to that person?

Answers

Part One. Reading Comprehension

1. Paulo pushed Sara Mendez down and ran away.

2. Because Sara Mendez said that Joaquim was a silly old man.

3. Joaquim suggested that Paulo apologize to Sara.

4. He felt a little better after apologizing to Sara.

 旅遊導覽

維德角共和國 (Republic of Cape Verde)

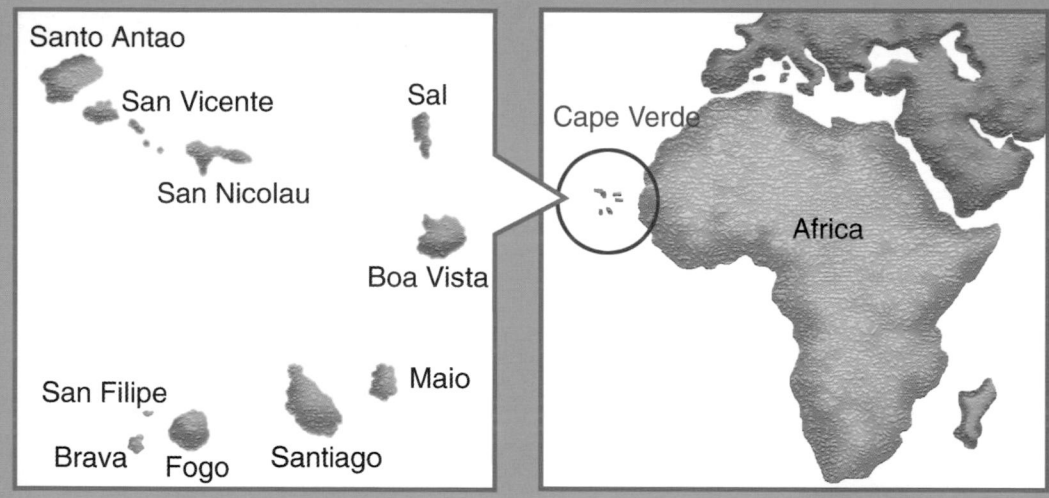

葡萄牙人發現
維德角群島

維德角群島被納入
葡萄牙殖民地版圖

因為殖民地及地緣關
係，維德角變成黑奴販
賣交易中心

因為旱災不斷，造成逾 10 萬人
死亡，黑奴人口銳減重挫維德角
殖民地的經濟

| 1456 年 | 1462 年 | 16 世紀 | 18-19 世紀 |

人口組成：

維德角共和國位於北大西洋西非洲突出部分之外海，主要是由十個大島組成。

在西元 1456 年葡萄牙人發現維德角群島之前，這裡是杳無人居的。成為葡萄牙的殖民地之後，原本居住在西非沿岸的黑人被大量引進這裡，幫助葡萄牙人開墾土地；再加上其他歐洲國家的人移居此地，多個種族混居的結果，除了有極少數純正的葡萄牙人之外，維德角大部分的人口是非洲人及歐洲人的混血後裔，少部分為非洲人。

自古以來維德角的自然資源匱乏並時常遭逢旱災，在生存困難的情況下，維德角獨立後居民紛紛移居海外。根據統計，擁有維德角血統的人口超過一百萬，但真正定居在維德角群島的卻只有三分之一的人口。大部分維德角後裔定居在美國東北部，葡萄牙、義大利及法國也有他們的蹤跡，更有一部分的後裔在非洲塞內加爾落腳。

簡單的短句	
英文	Crioulo
Yes.	Sin.
No.	Nau.
Excuse me.	Da-n lisensa.
Thank you.	Obrigadu.
Good morning.	Bon dia.
Good afternoon.	Boa tardi.
Good evening.	Bo noiti.

語言：

由於曾是葡萄牙殖民地，維德角共和國的官方語言是葡萄牙語。除此之外，當地還通行一種叫 Crioulo 的語言，是葡萄牙語跟非洲語混合所產生的語言。

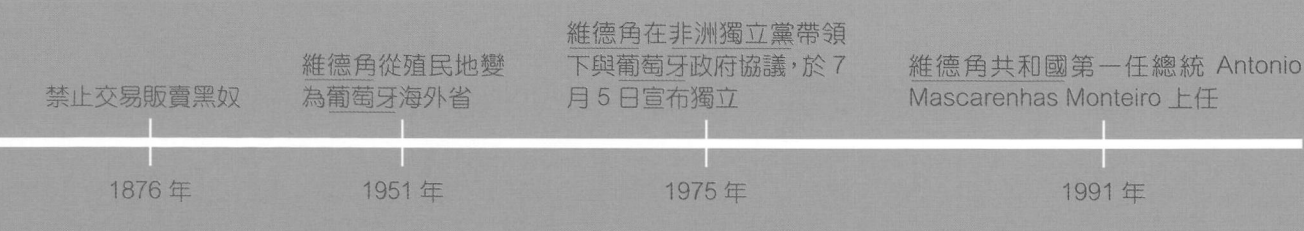

禁止交易販賣黑奴
1876 年

維德角從殖民地變為葡萄牙海外省
1951 年

維德角在非洲獨立黨帶領下與葡萄牙政府協議，於 7 月 5 日宣布獨立
1975 年

維德角共和國第一任總統 Antonio Mascarenhas Monteiro 上任
1991 年

About the Author

Born March 15th, 1969 in Laguna Beach, Christian Beamish has always been attracted to the water. His father introduced him to the ocean at a very young age and he has been surfing for more than 25 years. In 1987, after graduating high school, Christian joined the U.S. Navy and worked in a construction battalion on many overseas  projects. His Navy travels have been a very important part of his development as a writer since he was exposed to many interesting places and people. The time he spent in Cape Verde with the Navy was the basis for the Paulo and Joaquim stories: the unique culture of the islands and the way the people there are so closely connected to the sea. Christian currently lives in San Clemente, California and has plans to build an 18-foot sailboat for the next stage of his ocean development.

Author's Note: About *The Apology*

I wanted Paulo to have to face something that he'd done wrong. The more I imagined this little boy, the more real he became to me. I wanted him to have to deal with a problem, to learn how to accept responsibility for doing something wrong. With the help of his old friend Joaquim, Paulo begins to see things more clearly. I've been very fortunate to have befriended some people who are much older than myself, and I've often turned to them for their experience when I have a problem.

關於繪者

朱正明

1959 年次，現居台北市。

年幼好塗鴉；自高中時期即選讀美工科，業畢次年 (1979) 考取國立藝術專科學校美術科西畫組，1982 年以西畫水彩類第一名畢業。

求學時期除水彩、素描技法之外，並對漫畫、卡通之藝術表現形式頗有興趣，役畢後工作項度側重於卡通、漫畫、插畫。

1999 年驟生再學之念，並於次年考取國立師範大學美術研究所西畫創作組；2003 年取得美術碩士學位，該年申請入師大附中實習教師獲准，次年 2004 年取得教育部頒發之美術科正式教師資格證書，目前仍為自由工作者身分。

愛閱雙語叢書

(具國中以上英文閱讀能力者適讀)

祕密基地系列

Paulo, Joaquim and the Lighthouse Series

Christian Beamish　著
吳泳霈　譯
朱正明　繪
中英雙語，全套五本，附英文朗讀CD

①Crazy Joaquim　瘋子喬昆
②Paulo Joins the Fleet　第一次捕魚
③The Apology　保羅的道歉
④Homecoming　歸來
⑤The Blue Marlin Festival　藍馬林魚節

一段發生在西非的島嶼上，關於友誼與成長的故事。

在西非外海小島上的海邊漁村，矗立著一座
燈塔。燈塔管理員是一個叫喬昆的獨居老
人，村民們都誤以為他是個瘋子，但八歲
的小男孩保羅卻和他成為忘年之交，並學
到許多人生哲理。本系列五個溫馨且具
啟發性的生活事件，紀錄喬昆和保羅的
友誼。清新雋永的文字，配上細緻優
美的插畫，值得您細細品味。

愛閱雙語叢書

世界故事集系列

你想知道，
如何用簡單的英文，
說出一個個耳熟能詳的故事嗎？

本系列改編自世界各國民間故事，
讓你體驗以另一種語言呈現
你所熟知的故事。

Jonathan Augustine 著

Machi Takagi 繪

Bedtime Wishes
睡前願望

The Land of the
Immortals
仙人之谷

國家圖書館出版品預行編目資料

The Apology:保羅的道歉 / Christian Beamish著;朱
正明繪;吳泳霈譯.－－初版一刷.－－臺北市:三
民,2005
面; 公分.－－(愛閱雙語叢書.祕密基地系列③)
ISBN 957–14–4330–1 (精裝)

1.英國語言－讀本

524.38   94012750

網路書店位址 http://www.sanmin.com.tw

© The Apology
—— 保羅的道歉

著作人　Christian Beamish
繪　書　朱正明
譯　書　吳泳霈
發行人　劉振強
著作財
產權人　三民書局股份有限公司
　　　　臺北市復興北路386號
發行所　三民書局股份有限公司
　　　　地址／臺北市復興北路386號
　　　　電話／(02)25006600
　　　　郵撥／0009998–5
印刷所　三民書局股份有限公司
門市部　復北店／臺北市復興北路386號
　　　　重南店／臺北市重慶南路一段61號
初版一刷　2005年8月
編　號　S 805681
定　價　新臺幣貳佰元整
行政院新聞局登記證局版臺業字第〇二〇〇號

有著作權·不准侵害

ISBN　957–14–4330–1　(精裝)